SO-BYN-079

Clean Up Time

written by Pam Holden
illustrated by Kelvin Hawley

1

We clean up the
tables and the floor.

2

We clean up
the paints and
the brushes.

4

5

We clean up
the scissors and
the glue.

7

We clean up
the paper and
the crayons.

9

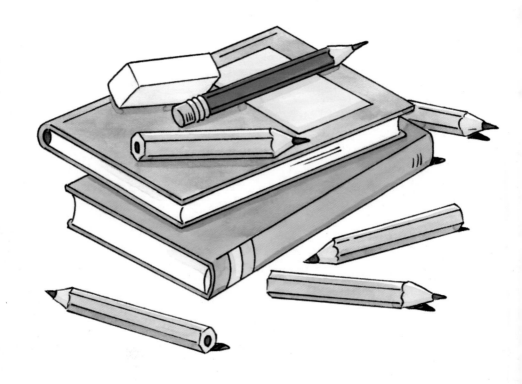

We clean up
the books and
the pencils.

10

11

We clean up the blocks and the toys.

13

We clean up
our hands.

15

We go out to play.

16